THE PRIVILEGE OF MEN

Judith Mazzucco

The Privilege of Men
(2nd Edition)
Copyright © 2019 by Judith Mazzucco
Cover design by Judith Mazzucco
Cover © 2019 by Judith Mazzucco
Author's photograph by Pablo Maitia

ISBN: 9781709136702
Imprint: Independently published
Printed and bound in the United States of America

This story is dedicated to all sentient beings who have been stripped bare of their very essence, all for the privilege of men.

Preface
Interspecies relationships are heartwarming and heartbreaking. Intra-species relationships are even more complicated. The relationships between men, women and animals can be reprehensible, especially when the mistreatment of women and animals coincides with ego and money.

Chapter 1

"Coffee or Tea?"

Kendra woke with a start. She had been dreaming. It took her a second or so to shake the dreams. She shifted in her seat, taking another split second to realize where she was. She gazed blankly at the flight attendant.

"Uhmmm, tea please."

"Would you like cream and sugar?" The flight attendant inquired. "Neither, thank you. Black is fine." Kendra settled back in her seat, relaxing and stretching as best she could. Sitting three across on a long haul flight is no fun at all, especially when you have to sleep elbow to elbow with a stranger.

Kendra had sat, before boarding the plane, in the members only lounge at the airport, enjoying a glass of wine with crackers. Once a year she received a lounge pass as a perk from her credit card company. Slouching low in her armchair with her feet propped up on the corner of the glass and iron table in front of her, she took a sip, and then another, feeling the mild burn of a first glass of wine as it descended into her stomach. She looked at the travelers around her: families, businesswomen and men, couples and a few lone travelers like herself. She began a little self-analysis; she could be removed and coldly analytical about herself when necessary.

She asked herself, "So why am I alone?"

"Good question," she replied.

Kendra interrupted her own conversation and began to think. While traveling all over the world she had certainly met numerous wonderful and attractive people and had experienced her fair share of romantic and lustful encounters, affaires if you wish, sounds a bit sexier. However, she had never slowed down to reflect on them, never changed a ticket nor postponed a flight because of any dalliance. She just kissed them goodbye and boarded the plane, never looking back. It was as if she was in a constant rush forward, always moving on to the next assignment, next story, next country, next adventure, next friend, next lover. At times she felt like the protagonist in one of Charles Aznavour's songs. "I ran so fast, that at last, time and youth ran out…" When would she finally let herself slow down?

She had recently retired from the BBC news desk in New York, intending to write free-lance, do a little research, and catch up with friends on long overdue visits. Her next goal was perhaps a Pulitzer, just perhaps, maybe. She always had to have a plan, something next in the hopper.

Kendra felt she had led a life of privilege. Money and privilege were not synonymous to her. Money was not of the utmost importance. It certainly made things easier, but as far as privilege was concerned, it was not the end all. She had a university education and had been gainfully employed, making her self-sufficient, all of which resulted in self-confidence. She could also travel freely anywhere in the world. That equated to privilege to Kendra. However, these were her rights as a woman to enjoy, actually rights that women everywhere in the world should be able to enjoy.

There was a time, when she was a girl, that she was intrigued with the fact that some people had friends in different parts of the world. In her child's mind, she had no idea how this could come to pass. Where and how did you find these friends, she wondered? At the age of ten, her frame of reference was still her immediate family and her friends at school, all of whom lived within a five-mile radius. Now that she had people she could actually call friends all over the world, she felt extremely smug and pleased with herself. There are people whose goals are to accumulate possessions, riches and wealth; Kendra's goal was to have these precious treasures scattered near and far. She felt extremely rich. She didn't have to contact them frequently. They needn't contact her often. Just knowing they were there for her made Kendra feel content and happy.

For many years she had lived in a house on Vandeventer Avenue in Princeton and commuted by train into Manhattan. It was a century old house that reflected the character of the leafy street of which it was a part. However, Kendra had always felt just as at home in Europe as in the States. Her friend Martine, who lived in northern Germany, once remarked that she should immigrate to Europe so they could see each other more often. She suggested Kendra should really live in the UK, so she need not worry about learning a new language. Kendra had many talents, but an affinity for languages was not one of them. Martine's statement had tempted and intrigued Kendra and she filed it away in the little Rolodex in the side of her brain. She thought that one day she might surprise herself and act upon the idea. However, she was not sure if she could tolerate the constant precipitation in the UK, the raw, bone-chilling weather, day in and day out. Eventually however, she could not resist the temptation of Martine's suggestion. Putting aside the harsh reality of the weather, she made the decision to try life in the Cotswolds for a while.

The plane landed in an early morning drizzle of a chilly and gray Glasgow. Kendra pulled up the collar of her Barbour coat and adjusted her scarf as she left the airport terminal and walked toward the taxi queue. She stood patiently waiting in the light rain, tired from the overnight flight. Kendra liked flying from Newark to England via Glasgow. She had friends in Glasgow and had come to really enjoy the energy of the city. She used to take a flight down to London for work. Now she would take a train to Birmingham to get to the Cotswolds. She took the train because it was impossible to fit a good size carry-on bag into the overhead compartment of the low cost Inter-European airlines and she refused, on principle, to pay to check a bag. She was looking forward to catching up with her Glasgow friend. They were meeting for tea at The Willow Tea Room, her favorite place. Later she would take the train south; she was eager to see what lay in store for her in England.

Settling into the taxi, she exchanged pleasantries with the driver. The radio was on. Headlining the news, was what seemed to Kendra, the daily dose of misfortune from around the world: India's seemingly constant violence against women, a Swedish tourist raped, a photojournalist beaten by a gang of men, and a teenager abducted. Kendra thought to herself, "What a way to start the day."

Chapter 2

The cottage, which she had found through an Internet source, was really picture perfect, except that there was no front yard, path or even step, as in: you couldn't open the front door because the road was there, RIGHT THERE! Fortunately, the back of the house was lovely. She just had to remember in the future that everything looks wonderful online. She wanted a cozy place where she could read by the fire on a rain soaked afternoon with a ginger colored cat curled up at her feet. She referred to this cat as the philosopher's cat. The image David Wood described, in his essay *Following Derrida*, had for years called to her and stayed with her. He wrote, "I am here and now, my ginger cat purring at my feet, in England, writing these words."

When Kendra arrived at the cottage from Glasgow, she brought tea and shortbread with her. She put them in the kitchen cupboard and looked around. That was the extent of her provisions. She eventually needed to get a car, but for the time being the bicycle in the shed behind the cottage would suffice. She also knew she needed to muster up the courage to tackle the round-a-bout by bike; lorries and busses quite frankly stopped her heart, but that would be for another day. She just felt too drained to think of it at the moment. A taxi would suffice. Sitting in the back of the taxi she put together a mental shopping list: food, wine, bread for toast, candles, matches and a few other odds and ends.

A few days later, Kendra travelled to visit an ex-colleague. He lived on a farm between Cambridge and New Market. Previously he had lived in the States for many years, then in India. Bryce was an interesting fellow. He had retired to the UK after a long stint behind the BBC Delhi news desk. India had always intrigued him. Kendra, on the other hand, found it intolerably crowded, hot and dirty. The other problem she had with India was the lack of laws supporting the rights of women and children. She was however, captivated by the colors and fine cotton produced in the country which, sadly came with the price of child labor.

Bryce and Kendra spent the afternoon together exchanging old gossip, catching up with current affairs, and other topics that captured their fancy. He never seemed to bring the conversation around to what was happening in Delhi at the moment. So, Kendra did. India was in the headlines and the news constantly. The caste system was still taking its toll on university students, killing themselves because of the anxiety and pressure of trying to fit in socially and academically. High-rise apartment buildings were being built in cities with no infrastructure to support them; there were numerous buildings built with literally no structural support at all. Corruption was ubiquitous. The atrocities committed toward women and girls were incomprehensible in civilized society. Kendra went on and on. When she got on a roll with something, especially a topic about which she was passionate, she could talk for hours, and then just fall in a heap, exhausted. "... And another interesting thing," she continued " No, I shouldn't say interesting, terrifying and sad is more like it, are the girls who disappear. Just gone. Here now. Then gone. Never to be seen or heard from again. It's on the news now all the time." Bryce interjected, "But girls run away and disappear all over the world, all the time. Sometimes they just don't want to be where they are and they leave." He wanted to change the subject. She saw that he was visibly disturbed.

Bryce loved India while he lived there, but for him it was over. He had moved on. Finally, Kendra looked out the window of the greenhouse conservatory where they were sitting, enjoying the early spring sunshine and the warmth it brought with it. Her mind wandered. She looked at the ewes and their lambs on the hillside that sloped away from the house. There was nothing sweeter than those babies, leaping into the air as if propelled by springs in their little legs.

"You look tired and distracted," Bryce remarked to Kendra. "I think its just jet lag catching up with me," she replied. "No matter how often I fly to Europe from the States, I always feel I can beat it, jet lag that is; but it always, by the third day, comes and smacks me right between the eyes."

The perils and passions of India had caught Kendra's attention, but only briefly. She was anxious to go home to her cottage and get some much-needed sleep. She looked forward to seeing where she would end up after being idle for a time. She left Bryce with promises to keep in touch.

It was very late when she got in. Bryce had invited her to stay over; she was grateful for the invite, but, she liked waking up in the morning in the place she wanted to be for the day, and that was the cottage. She finished a quick, late dinner and sipped the last of her wine. Staring at the candle flame, mesmerized, she wondered what would happen to her, if she would always be alone. She was thinking, merely thinking.

She crawled into her bed made up with sheets of soft Egyptian cotton, smelling faintly of lavender. She stretched and turned on her side, savoring the deliciousness of the moment. She stopped thinking about herself and started thinking about the girls, the girls who disappeared in India. She fell asleep thinking about them, and she woke up thinking about them. On the news each morning it had become almost commonplace to hear of girls and young women in India disappearing. Their plight gnawed at her. She was thinking about them more and more. As a matter of fact, she could not stop thinking about them. Kendra was starting to feel that these missing girls were consuming her every thought.

Chapter 3

Veronica had just walked into the house. Her run along the beach on the shore of New Jersey's Delaware Bay had been more difficult than usual. The winds were gusting, the kind of gusts that take your breath away. She was tall. Her blond hair was more on the gray side than blond, and she was in decent shape. She spoke passable French and was a complete and unabashed Francophile. If she had married for money, she would have been a regular at Sotheby's when a Van Gogh went under the hammer.

She began shedding her running clothes: first her shoes by the door, then her socks. Next she stretched her bra over her head and flung it into the washer, followed by her running tights. Before heading upstairs for a shower, she flicked on the electric teakettle. On the stairs she passed her husband, who commented, "nice outfit."

"Thanks, sweetie," she replied.

"You may be interested in an email that just came in for you," he said.

After showering she sat down at her computer with a cup of tea. The message was from Kendra. Veronica and Kendra worked together many years ago and had become fast friends immediately. They now saw each other rarely but their friendship was constant. Veronica sat back in her chair chewing on the earpiece of her reading glasses, reading and thinking.

Kendra had emailed Veronica the evening before, telling Veronica about her afternoon with Bryce, recounting the highs and lows of their conversation, including part of her discourse about abuse of power in India and the abhorrent disappearance of girls there. Kendra knew Veronica would want to pass on to their mutual friend Pat, the news of Bryce and all the gossip. Pat, had worked with Bryce, and liked him a lot. She thought he was intelligent, scholarly, well read and well travelled, but down deep could be a real bastard.

Pat and Veronica spoke to each other by phone every Sunday afternoon. The entire topic of conversation that particular Sunday was Bryce's time in India. As Pat shed light on Bryce's family situation while there, Veronica got goose bumps. Bryce's wife Celia had a daughter who disappeared about 15 years ago. Whether she had been kidnapped, abducted or run away was never known. Various investigations and searches led nowhere.

Veronica and Kendra always liked sending post cards, prosaic perhaps, but also nostalgic. This, however, was not a time for sentimentality. She immediately texted Kendra, "call or WhatsApp me, ASAP."

Moments later Kendra called.

"Listen to this," she said to Kendra. "It turns out Bryce had a daughter who disappeared."

"Are you kidding? He never mentioned a word of that to me!"

"Well, there it is. That's what Pat told me."

"Do you think that she just ran away from home? Kids do that all the time," Kendra said, parroting Bryce's earlier comment.

"No one has any idea what happened to her," said Veronica.

Kendra shuddered. She now knew why he had been so uncomfortable when the subject was broached.

Chapter 4

Pat had worked for many years with Bryce and retired shortly after he did. She knew him well. Pat was smart, quick-witted and had an outrageous sense of humor. She could be outright filthy and as funny as could be, but, somehow was always able to get away with it.

It was early evening by the time Pat got off the phone with Veronica and she immediately put in a call to Bryce, time zone differences be damned. Bryce answered sleepily.

"Bryce here."

"You old codger, how are you?"

"Nice of you to call, Pat. I wasn't doing anything but sleeping."

"You can sleep when you are dead. Heard you had a visitor-Kendra. I didn't know she was spending time in England."

"Well, Pat, I'm sorry you didn't get her memo that she would be out of the country for awhile. Yes, she stopped by. I like her. She is smart and has a dry sense of humor. She is good company, too. So, what's going on?"

"I just thought I would give you a heads up so you can get your self emotionally ready," Pat continued.

"How so?"

Pat went on to explain that Kendra and Veronica were becoming intrigued, curious and disgusted with the frequency of cases of missing girls and women in India.

Chapter 5

Bryce spent many years in India. He was married to Celia, a photojournalist who had a daughter. Neither of them returned with him to England.

Celia was everything a man could want and everything a woman could fantasize being. She was a lovely blond, born in Mexico City and educated in the US. The blond hair may or may not have been in her DNA, but she certainly was stunning. She graduated from law school, but her only real interest was photojournalism. This led her to the colors, contrasts, beauty and horrors of India.

Celia's daughter was abducted on her way home from school one afternoon. That was fifteen years ago on The Girl's 16th birthday. Immediately after school was the time of day that provided the most opportunity for predators. Students stayed late at school. Parents stayed later at work. An hour or two before realizing a child was missing gave the abductors the much-needed time to escape with their prizes. The trains, buses and roadways were crowded at rush hour and no one gave a second look at a man traveling with a young girl. All forms of public transportation were packed to the point of incomprehensibility by Western standards. The girls were threatened, frightened, and probably had a knife pressed against their lower ribs. They offered little resistance.

Bryce had convinced himself that The Girl was not his daughter; he was positive and cared little about her. When Celia told Bryce that The Girl had been abducted, at first he was shocked, but then he felt a wave of relief swell over him. He felt guilty at first for feeling this way, but also a release from being shackled to a child he believed was not his. Perhaps it might have been different if Celia had confessed an indiscretion to him. No, it would not have changed anything. All he ever felt for The Girl was resentment. Then he grew to not only resent Celia, also, but then to loathe her. He would not divorce her. He would only give her nothing, no divorce, no settlement, and no estrangement. He wanted her to suffer. And suffer she did.

When Bryce was in his twenties, he was out on his family's farm tracking down stray sheep. It was a typical sloppy UK weather day. Bryce was wearing old worn Wellies with very little tread left on the sole. He had climbed a wooden board fence to cross it. The wood was wet and slick. As he swung his leg over, straddling the fence, his foot slipped and he came down hard, crushing his testicles on the fence. A doctor later gave him the grim news that he would never be able to father children.

That being said, the fact was that Bryce had one blue and one brown eye, Heterochromia iridium, a relatively uncommon coloring of the eyes. Celia's daughter had one blue and one brown eye. Against all logic, Bryce was in complete denial that The Girl could ever be his daughter.

After her daughter disappeared, Celia stayed in India as long as she could bear it. The heartache became too much for her. She had tried in vain to find her only daughter, following each and every possible lead, all to no avail. Her frustration and anger mounted day by day. Bryce had also looked long and hard. Each time he had come back to her empty-handed, reporting that he had found no leads, nothing at all. Eventually, they would leave India. Bryce felt they must pick up the pieces and carry on. Bryce was looking forward to returning to England; but Celia was not. It was too far and too final. She needed someplace hospitable where her heart could, if not mend, at least stop hemorrhaging. She found solace in Perth, Australia. In her emotional mind's eye, it was in the same half of the world as India, giving her some distance and perspective, but close enough to be there, just in case.

Chapter 6

It had been a long day. Every day was a long day for Valdez. He got to the school early and stayed late tutoring students who wanted or needed extra help. He felt fortunate. He loved teaching and was glad he had returned to it. That was a long time ago and far away, but it was paying off now. He was also happy he had returned to his birthplace.

His current job was teaching Spanish at the High School in La Lucila, a suburb of Buenos Aires, Argentina. The school was private, very private. Every year he seemed to get a student who became a special project. There was always drama, always a story.

But, for now he was in the States attending a seminar at Princeton University on Latin American Literature, his favorite subject area. He went into the hardware store on Nassau Street, looking for a bungee cord to be added to his carry-on. He wanted to wrap one around his suitcase and slip his jacket through it while he was waiting at the airport so everything would be in one place. He grew tired of things "gone missing" when he traveled.

It was the week before Kendra was to leave for the UK and she was in the same store having a spare set of keys made for the graduate students who would be renting her house and buying a stopper for her antique claw footed bathtub. By the expression on her face Valdez knew she had a question about which one to buy, so he made a suggestion.

As they left the store, he held the door for her. He was such a gentleman and so disarmingly nice. She smiled and thanked him. He asked if she could recommend a place for a drink since he was not familiar with the town, and would she like to join him? She looked at him quizzically. A drink at this hour, she thought. He read her expression and replied. "You don't have to take it so literally. A tea or a coffee perhaps, and actually it must be the cocktail hour someplace in the world." To her surprise, she acquiesced.

Chapter 7

Jerome was Kendra's oldest friend. They had studied at the same university together and shared a long history. Jerome had always followed the money. This served him well in the past, but only the past. Times were changing. He swore now he should have gone into teaching instead of cosmetology. He worked as a hair stylist. The money trail had led him from Northern New Jersey, to New York City and finally to Richmond Hill in the UK. He was probably the best colorist on either or both sides of the Atlantic. It was his background as an artist that gave him that creative edge, making him sought after and well known.

Jerome came home late; the procession of women through the salon had been endless. But now he was finally done, done, done, really done for the day. He kicked off his butter soft Italian loafers by the door, took two steps and immediately deposited his bags on the hall table. A glass filled with ice and vodka loomed large in his mind. He opened the china cabinet and retrieved a heavy cut glass tumbler, one of those classic leaded crystal 1930's "rocks" glasses; so beautiful to look at and so deadly to use.

Kendra and Jerome knew each other better than almost anyone else. Theirs was an unqualified friendship. Each took the other at absolute face value with total unconditional love, dog like. Their friendship was a treasure of which each was cognizant.

Chapter 8

Kendra's days at her new cottage began with her usual routine of exercise, tea, toast and the news. Unfortunately, the morning's news contained two more dreadful stories: the first, a student raped and beaten, and the second, another disappearance of young girls.

Kendra tried to focus on what was around her. She wanted to get out and about to learn the lay of the land around her new home and get the feel of the community. There were the pubs, the library, an Oxfam consignment shop, and the market, all surrounded by farms. It was almost picture perfect. She needed to do some clothes shopping at the thrift shop since she had brought very little with her. She had indeed become a fanatic for travelling with carry-on only. Basically, it had become sport to her. The less the better, that was the challenge.

She had looked forward to being in the beautiful Cotswolds countryside for so long and now that she was there, oddly enough, her thoughts were elsewhere. Everything around her began to seem superficial and meaningless. Kendra tried to sort through what her feelings and thoughts were. She realized that she was becoming obsessed with these young women in India whom she did not know but heard about on the daily news. She could not make herself ignore them any longer. Instead of fighting the duality of what was going on inside herself, she decided to take a step back and embrace it. She realized what she needed to do was some research and to organize her thoughts. Systematically she went through all the information she found. She categorized and cross-referenced everything. Once she started the process she realized just how deep her commitment to this investigation was becoming.

She shared all her research with Veronica. There were a lot of articles and newscasts, but not much hard information or facts to go on. Kendra remarked, "The only thing I do know is that no one really knows where the girls are all ending up. I'm sure some are sold as slaves and as for the others, there is a big market for sex workers in Mumbai. That used to be referred to as the Cages of Bombay."

"Do you think Bryce's daughter was kidnapped to work there?" asked Veronica.

"I don't know. Even as terrible a fate as those poor girls have, they used to eventually, some of them at least, return home or escape. But something else seems to be happening at present. The girls who disappear now are simply vanishing without a trace. They never surface again," replied Kendra.

They both researched the known possibilities of where young girls could be hidden, the sex trade, the Cages of Bombay and human trafficking. They knew what hell lay to the south, but might there be something else going on, perhaps to the north?

Kendra remarked to Veronica, "When I think about what I have done or not done in my life, I find I only regret what I have not done. I don't want to look back ten years from now and regret not doing what we could have done to help find these girls." They realized their goal was now to try and solve this mystery and perhaps to help Celia find her daughter.

Kendra recognized the fact that she could work from afar for only so long. She needed to go to India. She did not embrace the idea. Going there would be expensive and dangerous. She knew she could not operate there by herself; she needed backup and support. Could she convince any of her friends to drop everything and go to India with her? This would mean putting their normal lives on hold, even borrowing money if necessary, and flying to India to search for girls who had dissolved into phantoms.

Kendra started to make a list of people: Veronica, Greta, Jerome, and Martine. A party list it was not. She realized this was not how she had originally envisioned getting together with her old friends. Nevertheless, it was what it was and she was going to have to run with it. Kendra's friends were people of privilege…privilege not that they were born into, but earned with an education that provided them with opportunity. They were not affluent, but the money they earned did make them independent.

They could do what they wanted, when they wanted, without asking someone else to pay for it. They never abused the privilege. They enjoyed their privilege, but they also used it to benefit others less fortunate. Those deemed less fortunate were of all shapes, sizes and species.

Kendra vetted each one of her friends at great length. She was not sure Veronica was without question 100% on board. Jerome would take some coaxing. On the other hand, Martine was always up for an adventure. Greta would be the really tough nut to crack. As Kendra contacted each one, inviting, urging and begging them to come, she knew she had to tell them to bring money, a lot of it. She hoped they would be comfortable with the request. Usually friendship and a request for money are not a desirable mix, with the friendship suffering and becoming unsustainable.

Kendra and Veronica discussed their reasons for their involvement. Veronica thought that perhaps it would be a way to assuage her feeling of guilt for not taking more positive positions in the past. Years ago, her sister had been raped on her drive home from college. Her car had a flat tire and the man who stopped to help her abused her. Afterward, she continued home and nothing came of it. The police were called, but neither her parents nor the police pursued it. The offender remains at large to this day. This surfaces in Veronica's conscience from time to time.

There were other instances of regret when Veronica started digging deeper. A colleague who worked for her was married to a physically abusive man and another colleague was married to a man who mentally and verbally abused her. Veronica felt helpless in both situations. Each woman accepted the situation as if this was her lot in life and it was how her life was to be. They did not seek help; they were not sure how. Each just tried to cope. One is still married; the other finally got a divorce. However, Veronica felt her hands were tied as to any intervention in each of the circumstances because police were not always sympathetic to rape victims, parents did not want their names publicized, and many woman are held hostage by abusive husbands almost voluntarily.

17

Veronica always thought she was doing the right thing but going to a country with a purpose other than being a tourist might put more soul into her already meaningful life. It might put another notch in her humanity-helping belt. She concluded that this indeed would be a fulfilling endeavor for her.

Martine was well, how to put it, she was Martine. She was indeed the recipient of a privileged life. Martine had studied linguistics at both German and American universities and spoke several languages. Kendra and she met, years ago, while sharing a bench at lunchtime in Washington Square Park. She was studying translation at NYU. She was highly educated, could have gotten a job most anywhere in the world, but the only thing she really wanted to do was to ride horses. She was a very talented and successful rider. Her family bred, raised and showed fine German Warmblood horses in the north of Germany. She loved her rural life, but she also liked to travel. Martine never needed an excuse for an adventure. A few years ago she rode in a 600-mile horse race across Mongolia.

She considered the "India Project", as she had christened it, an adventure with a cause. She just needed to get coverage for herself on the farm, someone to feed and care for her horses; and then she was as good as there already.

Greta was a dog behaviorist and a professional dog trainer, who lived on the East Coast of the United States, a few hours drive from Veronica. She trained all types of canines, from wolves for the cinema, search and rescue dogs, to household companions. Most of her own dogs were raised from puppies and trained to be the best. Hopefully she would be able to provide the "security forces" that would be needed in India. Kendra knew Greta would be hard pressed to make the trip, but it was worth a try to convince her. Greta hated to travel. She was intelligent, well educated, fiercely independent, and refused to read fiction. Greta was tough, real no nonsense, tall, attractive and could be slightly intimidating. She had been married a few times and was now a serial Internet dater. Kendra made the comment "He seems nice..." after Greta described her latest boyfriend.

Greta replied, "They are all nice, until you get to know them."

Kendra felt that if she played the sympathy card of the missing girls to the hilt, Greta might cave. To Kendra's relief, she eventually came through because dogs were essential to this endeavor. Each woman would always travel with a dog, her ultimate protector. There would be no victims here. They each would have a canine companion with them at all times. The women would never be portrayed as vulnerable. The dogs, however, needed to be ragtag looking canines of ill repute, Indian street dogs or "Village Dogs" as John Bradshaw refers to them. Nothing should stand out and draw unwanted attention.

Chapter 9

The whole investigation started to materialize and "The India Project" was set in motion. The plan was for the entourage to fly into Delhi then go directly from the airport and check into the Imperial Hotel and get a good night's rest after their long flights. Kendra always lived by Robert Ludlum's words, "Sleep is your best defense." The next morning the transformations would begin at the first apartment Kendra had rented for them.

Kendra felt the best way for her and the other women to travel safely and freely in India would be to assume the characteristics and personas of men, look, dress and act like men. Actually they would become androgynous. They would cut their hair, dye it black, apply a bronze tint to their skin, wear men's clothing and constantly don sunglasses. Kendra had, in the past, tried unsuccessfully to wear contact lenses. She knew dark colored contact lenses would be best, however, for her they were out of the question. Sunglasses would have to suffice. Kendra also insisted that everyone be micro-chipped with their vitals: Passport number, Social Security number, etc. The chip was discreetly implanted in each person in the fleshy area next to the armpit. This was not anticipating the worst; it was being prepared for anything and everything that might transpire.

The apartment's kitchen was being used as the salon; as each one emerged from it, they were taken aback, viewing their changes in the mirror. All sported cropped hair, dyed jet black with black eyebrows. Their next destination was the bathroom, where a spray booth had been hastily erected. Pragmatism was the mantra, as long as it worked and did the job, that was all that mattered. Again each emerged, further altered. This time they all reflected an ocher, tan complexion. Jerome had worked his magic. He had transformed each into a generic Asian human, dressed in tan khaki pants or jeans, cotton shirt, sandals or old dusty canvas slip-on shoes.

The plan of action for "The India Project" was quite simplistic, it was observation. They would try to pay attention to all travelers and traffic as much as they could. They would keep an eye on bus stations, train stations, truck stops, anywhere men could be seen with girls. They needed to get the rhythm of the movement of the city. The girls had to be going somewhere. They were not just vanishing into thin air, or perhaps they were.

Tonight everyone would move, once again, to still another apartment, the one with the dogs. Their assimilation into the city was about to begin.

Chapter 10

Greta had been reticent to get involved with the purchase or adoption of dogs in India. The only things that came to her mind were the wire crates in the dog markets in Thailand and China. Dog upon dog smashed into the wire cages, where they were weighed and sold by the pound for meat. Kendra understood this, but urged her to reconsider. Both knew that it was not reasonable to bring trained dogs from the United States, because these dogs would stand out and draw attention to the women beside them. They had to calmly figure out their dog acquisition plan. Trying to be unemotional was the key. How they could re-purpose these unwanted, abused dogs into the dogs that would be their ultimate protectors would be Greta's crucial task. Kendra and Greta were going to be the saviors of the dogs involved; they decided to spread the salvation around. The dogs could come from the street, rescue agencies or meat markets. Greta swallowed hard and accepted her challenge.

She decided to ease herself into the process. She started with a rescue agency. When she entered the facility, the little snouts were pressed to the cage doors. They barked, "Pick me, pick me!!" A sea of tails was wagging. She selected two amiable, neutered souls. Nice and easy.

Now came the tough one, the dog meat market. Technically eating dogs was illegal in India; however, this was not the case everywhere in the country. To find the dog meat markets they would have to travel to the Northeastern states.

"Are we sure we really want to go to Nagaland?" queried Greta. "This is getting a little crazy. Maybe we should think about this," she continued.

"Of course it is crazy. This whole project is crazy. But if we think too long about it nothing will happen. Nothing will get done. Look, Greta," replied Kendra. "How about this, we get four dog crates, fly into Dimapur, go straight to the market and fly back with the dogs that night. We'll find a vet who will give the rabies shots that are needed to fly."

Greta sighed and then took a deep breath. "All right, let's do it."

Up until now both women had only seen the horror of the dog meat markets in pictures; the reality of it was shocking. "Although eating dogs is illegal in India, obviously these people have not gotten the memo," Greta lamented. The grills were fired up. Smoke was rising. The pungent smell of flesh cooking was everywhere. To Greta it was revolting; she thought she would throw up. She was glad Kendra had come with her. She didn't think she could face this alone. There were dogs in cages, others tied with ropes to grills and still others wrapped in burlap sacks, all oblivious to their immediate fates. She talked herself through the horror. She knew the dog tied to the grill would have to be her first project. The grill master was taken aback and surprised that Greta wanted the whole dog, NOT cooked. Money can buy anything. She exchanged rupees for the dog. He was untied and was now hers. The dog happily trotted along beside the two women, oblivious to his near fate. Kendra and Greta looked at each other, shook their heads and sighed. "This is REALLY horrible. I can't believe people and animals exist like this. Why do they feel they have the right to eat man's best friend? And if it is a cultural difference, then I ask who is their best friend here? Look at the eyes on these dogs, they are so loving and trusting. It breaks your heart. The inhumanity of it all is reprehensible," sighed Kendra.

They had purchased all the dogs they needed and were finally leaving the market. On the way out, by a wall of rock and stone, there was one last canine grill. A dog sat next to the wall wrapped in a burlap bag with only its head showing. The dog's eyes met Kendra's and Greta's. They then looked at each other. "I guess we can take one more," sighed Kendra, overwhelmed by the sadness of the sight. She offered a handful of rupees to the grill tender. He shrugged her off. She offered more. He became interested. The women looked at the dog, then the bag. The bag moved. Something was squirming inside it. No, this can't be, thought Kendra. She reached down and felt the bag. The grill man grabbed her arm. She jerked away from him. She gave him more rupees. He then shoved the dog in the bag toward her. She and Greta picked up the dog and the squirming burlap bag. Once they had left the market they put the dog down to examine it. They untied the string at the dog's neck and the bag fell away, revealing six plump puppies. They let the mother out of the bag, leaving the puppies confined to it. Kendra spun the top of the sack closed. She picked it up, holding the sack just high enough to allow the mother dog to smell her puppies and follow untethered. This was the last thing in the world they needed.

The veterinarian who helped them was wonderful; she even drove them to the airport and helped expedite getting the dogs in their crates and aboard the plane.

Fastening her seat belt, Greta looked at Kendra and remarked, "Wasn't it Gandhi who said something about the greatness of a nation and its morality can be judged by the way it treats its animals?"

"I believe so. It certainly rings true here," sighed Kendra.

All the dogs made a seamless transition from life on the fringe of society to life in the apartment. They were as nondescript looking as the humans they were with; their transformations were equally as remarkable. Greta got everyone on a training regimen and schedule. Life was one with the dogs. Everyone trained together, took the dogs for long walks together, and socialized with the dogs together. The hardest socialization event was trying to enjoy a tea and lachedar paratha, a butter-layered bread, without the dogs snatching it out of their hands. It had become everyone's favorite. Also evident was the fact that humans had nothing to do with domestication; dogs simply domesticated themselves. The dogs decided they were going to live with humans; the humans had to just stand back and let them in; otherwise, they would have broken down the door because they were coming into the lives of humans, like it or not. Dogs are both manipulative and cunning. They are the ones who have humans wrapped around their paws, the lucky ones.

Greta let each dog choose their person. In the midst of

the routine of socializing and training, to everyone's delight, the chaos of the puppies reigned supreme. Every time Jerome looked at the puppies, he shook his head; all he could think of was the alternate fate of these poor little creatures... "Puppies Panini."

Chapter 11

The surveillance started as soon as the dogs were ready. It would continue around the clock for weeks, with everyone recording their observations constantly. At the end of each day, they all came back to the apartment and compiled the data. Everything was referenced and cross-referenced. They spoke of everything they saw, things that mattered and didn't seem to matter. They had no real idea what they were looking for, so they just kept looking. They observed and video taped as much as they could, watching trains, buses, and trucks. The majority of young girls being hustled along with men were of two distinct types and going in opposite directions. Large-framed men with large-framed girls and young women were headed in a northern direction. Smaller, lighter framed men with small, more petite women were headed south. They knew the southern destination was most probably the Cages of Bombay. But what lay to the north? This was the puzzle.

Simone was an old friend of Kendra's who lived in Barcelona. From time to time she worked for the Spanish Department of Agriculture inspecting chickens imported from France. Here was poor Simone, a vegetarian, inspecting chickens for slaughter. She was always at odds with her personal morality. Kendra contacted her, hoping she could shed some light on the agricultural angle in India. Simone said the lush farmland that lay to the north and west always needed labor, but she hadn't heard of any "slave trade" of that sort. However she would ask around.

So there are farms, thought Kendra.

While on surveillance they always went out in twos, each person with a dog. They would visit the train stations and bus stations some days; other days they would take a car and drive to the end of the slums, where the masses of humanity ended, or at least thinned out. They would stop by the roadside, park their car, and drink tea from a vendor. They would also pay him more rupees than he would make in a month, so he was happy to ignore them.

Money could buy ignorance and bliss. The dogs watched, waited and dozed patiently beside them in the car. They watched the cars and the trucks. What exactly, besides young girls, they were looking for was unclear. The one thing that passed them the most frequently were trucks transporting pigs, goats, chickens. They made videos of everything and everybody.

Kendra and Jerome were sitting one morning by their favorite tea vendor in an old manual transmission Ford Fiesta. They were observing trucks, lots of them. Something odd stood out about one of the trucks carrying pigs. The pigs were all very high in the truck, even though it appeared to have only one level. They decided to follow it. As the truck headed out of town and the traffic grew thinner, they realized they needed a backup or at least a plan, neither of which they had. They drove at a good distance behind the truck. Occasionally, it slowed down. The third time it slowed they quickly passed it, continuing on as if a truck loaded with pigs meant nothing to them. They drove in silence, their mouths dry as cotton balls in a dust storm. They would let the truck follow them and simply watch to see if and when it left the highway. This went on for a few hours. They were driving due north. They drove over a mountain and a valley opened in front of them. Ahead lay a roadside truck stop selling petrol, tea and food. They pulled in. The truck they were "following" was well behind them. Jerome positioned the car behind a truck out of sight from the road. They both got out to stretch their legs and let the dogs have a chance to pee.

About ten minutes later, the truck with the pigs passed. Money was quickly exchanged for the gasoline and everyone piled into the car. Within moments, they were in quick pursuit of the pig hauler. Finally when the truck turned off the highway, it was onto a very narrow, dusty, barely two car wide road. Kendra and Jerome left the car parked on the side of the road and followed on foot. The dogs padded along silently at their sides. It was hot and dusty. They could feel the grit of the dust on their teeth. The grass beside the road was high enough that they could easily step into it and not be seen, if necessary. Up ahead were one-story concrete buildings, typical of many in this part of the world. You could not really tell or decide whether they were being built or falling apart.

They dared go no further and returned to the car, happy that they didn't have to venture into the tall grass with the possibility of encountering a snake or two or three....

On the drive back to the apartment, they decided that tomorrow Greta and Jerome, in a different car, would drink tea at the same vendor until they saw another possible truck to follow.

That evening they spoke to a friend of a friend of Veronica's who worked in the French consulate. They showed him on a map where they had been. He said there wasn't much out there besides mountains, hilly countryside and then farms, and some factory farms. Now they knew where the pigs had been going.

Greta and Jerome had just settled in to the surveillance when another unusually high truck with pigs in it passed them. Jerome nearly choked on his tea when he saw it. Greta immediately put the well-worn Tata motorcar in gear and casually let other vehicles get between the pig truck and themselves. This time they had a good idea where they were headed. Jerome and Greta saw in the distance the truck with the pigs turn off on the same road as the day before. However, what they would find today was much different than what the others saw the day before.

They parked well off the road, turning the car around to facilitate a quick get-away. After a short walk along the road, they noticed a pole and flag up ahead. When they reached it they noticed the tall grass pushed down. There was a small box attached to the side of the flagpole, presumably to leave money in. Greta and Jerome stared in disbelief at what lay next to the pole. There were two young water buffalo calves and two human babies on the side of the road. They all were bound, gagged and blindfolded, calves and babies. Were these offspring of two species being exchanged for money?

What ever they decided to do it would have to be swift and with a purpose. The two looked at each other. The children were a given, but what about the calves? Quickly Greta thrust the babies into Jerome's arms. The calves were more problematic. She decided the best way to get them to the car was to drag them, since they were too heavy for her to carry. The sand was soft and deep, even if the calves were scraped up a bit, it was better than the alternative that lay ahead for them at the factory farm. A purposeful walk was the fastest they could muster getting to the car. The back seat became an interspecies scramble of arms, legs and bodies. The dogs seeking refuge near the wheel well, graciously making room for the newcomers. Greta slammed the car into gear, bumping and going as fast as possible, terrified that another pig truck would enter the narrow road before they could reach the highway. Jerome was winded and felt sick with fright. The highway was only a few hundred feet ahead. Greta saw the lane of the highway coming up fast. Never letting up on the gas pedal, and glancing to her right, she sped onto the highway. No one said a word.

Kendra just shook her head when Greta and Jerome arrived at the apartment with the foundlings. Unbelievable, she thought, this was one more complication that was not needed. There had to be an animal sanctuary that would take the water buffalo calves, so that was good. Perhaps, with a sizable donation the babies could be placed in a convent, until she could figure out what was going on. Mother Theresa still had to have some good connections here, she thought. The one thing they could definitely not do was go to the police. Nobody played by the rules here.

Chapter 12

When the search branched out to the area north of Delhi, it was decided that more resources would be needed. If it became necessary to fly into this remote area, a pilot would be needed, basically a bush pilot, and a plane of course. Kendra had a pilot in mind; she thought they also might need a mechanic. She had a feeling that a mechanic would be an absolute necessity for everyone's safety.

Kendra emailed, then texted Valdez, asking him to call her. She felt that, when asking an almost stranger for a favor, it was better to speak with him personally. After exchanging pleasantries and telling him she was not in England, but in Delhi, and what she and her companions were doing, she explained why she needed a really good mechanic.

"A mechanic?"

"Yes, someone good to work on an airplane engine."

"Why did you think of me? I teach and trust me I do not have one mechanically oriented bone in my body," he replied.

"I realize that, but when we were at the restaurant in Princeton, and now I am not sure how or why it came up, you mentioned a friend of yours who had been a mechanic in the Merchant Marine in Buenos Aires," answered Kendra.

"Yes, I remember now. His name is Oscar and he CAN fix most anything, but I'm not sure about airplanes. He's living in New Jersey."

"Engines are all the same; engines on land, on water or in the air. Can you call him for me? I need him in Delhi. Probably by the end of the month or sooner."

"This is the end of the month."

"OK, then sooner."

"I'll talk to you later," and Valdez hung up.

Chapter 13

Nick hadn't seen or spoken to Kendra in years. They usually exchanged good wishes on each other's birthdays, but that was about it. Getting a text with an ASAP was out of the ordinary.

"So what's going on? How are you?" Nick offered.

"Fine. I'm fine, fine, fine," Kendra replied and continued. "Do you remember how you once made the comment that you would have no social life if it weren't for stray animals and lost causes?"

"Yeah, sounds like me."

"Well this is well suited for you, and besides, I need a pilot."

"I haven't flown in years."

"It's just like riding a bike, well almost, you never forget." Kendra proceeded to tell Nick what was going on in Delhi. She explained "The India Project" to him in complete detail. Told him about each person who was involved in the search and spoke of the dogs.

"Will you consider coming to Delhi?"

There was a slight hesitation and then more silence on Nick's end of the line. She could hear him breathing and thinking. Then his response came, "Hell yes. I'll go. There is fack-all happening here right now. Just have to arrange for my sister to take care of my dogs and cat for me. I'll work it out." Now it was Kendra's turn to breathe a sigh of relief. She gave him the coordinates of the areas so he could get aerial photographs of the terrain. "Let me do some homework, but off the top of my head I'll probably need a Cessna Caravan. But, I'll have to wait to see what is available there," he said.

"Hey, Nick, thanks."

"No problem. Now, what other information do you have for me?"

Kendra continued, "Do what ever you need to do and figure out what you need. Once in Delhi all it will take is money and you'll have the plane. Just let me know when you are coming.

When you make your reservation make it for two. You'll be flying in with your mechanic. I'd feel safer with our own mechanic, besides he can also keep these pieces of junk cars that we are driving going for us. Fly through Newark, deplane, get a taxi, and pick him up in Elizabeth and head back to the airport. I've been told he is a darling and a great mechanic, but he has no sense of direction, nor concept of time. He is Argentine. We can't afford for him to be late."

"So this is the real deal?" Nick asked.

"I've always been the real deal. You just never appreciated it."

Chapter 14

Watching for any signs of the missing girls had been going on for weeks. In the evenings, in the apartment, Kendra, Martine, Jerome and Veronica would review the day's videotapes. They were not sure what they were looking for, but knew they had to look for clues over and over again. Greta spent the time training the dogs. When everyone's eyes got tired, breaks were taken and the women were trained in concert with the dogs. The dogs caught on quickly; the women just had to be reminded to be consistent.

Jerome would touch up their "complexions" in the spray booth. One evening Kendra told Jerome her roots needed darkening. He suggested she wear a turban. Kendra did not feel this was an option, since a turban was a cultural icon, she would not use it as a costume. Jerome touched up her roots. He felt differently about the subject.

Some evenings Oscar stopped by to work on the cars. Nick came with him. Nick had opted for them to stay out near the airport where he could make better connections for the aircraft that was needed. When he came to the apartment he helped review the videos. Some nights things got crazy. The dogs would start barking and the humans got short tempered. This was one such night.

"Come here, give me a hug," Nick said to Kendra.

"No, STOP!"

"OK. OK. No biggie, just trying to be nice."

"No. Stop right there. Go Back!" They all looked at Kendra and then to the video footage she was viewing with Martine. It was one of the pig trucks they had all seen numerous times.

"Look, there," Kendra said, pointing at the computer screen. "Right at the space between the slats near the bed of the truck." There they saw it, a small human hand, grasping at anything, signaling, hoping to be seen.

"I can't believe it. They are right in front of us every day,"

Veronica sighed. Just then, Kendra's cell phone rang. "Bryce, good to hear from you. What's the weather like in New Market?"

"Haven't the foggiest, I'm here in Delhi," he replied. Kendra thought, what good fortune and perfect timing.

"Bryce, you're not going to believe this, but we think we know where some of these girls are disappearing to."

"Are you sure?" She was as sure as anyone could be.

"Did you find my daughter?"

"I don't know," she said. It came out as a whisper.

"I'm glad you're here," she continued. "You can come with us to the place where we think they are. Come out to the apartment tonight and we can fill you in on everything."

Kendra felt a wave of relief wash over her. At last they would have some help on the ground here in India. Hopefully Bryce could speak one of the dialects north of Delhi. The only dialect they all had been speaking so far was a monetary one, which had been well understood.

Chapter 15

Nick had stayed out at the airport for a reason, not to get away from the chaos of the apartment, but to try to make connections. It turned out that he and Oscar fit rather seamlessly into the international mix of pilots and maintenance mechanics at the cargo terminal and the private aviation hangers. To Nick's utter amazement, most everyone spoke English. It wasn't long before he and Oscar made the progression from drinking tea in the mornings with "the guys" to going out for beer in the evening. "The guys" turned out to be an interesting mix of ex-pats, adventurers, and private professional pilots.

On one such evening, when the subject of what exactly Nick and Oscar were doing in Delhi came up, Nick confessed that they had originally come to visit friends, but were now looking for a plane to head south to do some diving in remote areas. The Maldives was too "discovered" for their liking. One of "the guys" in the group pointed across the bar saying, "Abbi is the guy you should talk to. He used to fly a really sweet Otter in and out of here all the time. Tomorrow if you come by the hanger, you'll see it. Let's go over, I'll introduce you to him." They left the bar and approached the men's table, where two Indians and an Israeli, were seated. Introductions were made all around. The questions of "So, what brings you here?" and "How did you end up here?" were also exchanged.

"How does anyone end up anywhere?" Abbi commented. "It seems that it is always the same story, money and love, the lack of either or the prospect of both."

"That sounds familiar," replied Nick. "So, I hear you used to fly an Otter, my favorite," continued Nick. He thought to himself, either this fellow, Abbi picks up the conversation and runs with it or tells me to butt out and mind my own business.

"Let me tell you the story of what is going on with that plane," said Abbi.

"Let ME order another round of drinks for everyone before

you start," exhaled Nick.

It seemed that a wealthy businessman who had made his fortune in Agri-Business owned the plane. Abbi had flown it regularly for him up until recently. The man had suffered a stroke and was not able to do much of anything. Needless to say he wasn't going anywhere soon, couldn't fly and the plane sat idle.

"What a perfect plane for island hopping," said Nick. "Do you think he would lease it to me for a month or so?" Just throw it out there, thought Nick.

"Tell you what, I usually stop to visit him once a week. Why don't you come with me and you can ask him yourself. He isn't much to look at right now, but let me tell you, his wife is a REAL piece of eye candy," Abbi said. Nick hated that phrase.

The apartment of the businessman was in a new high-rise in a new type community for which India is famous. They bulldoze over farmland, turn farmers into paupers, and construct towering buildings with little to no infrastructure, either within the building or the community. Riding up to the apartment in the elevator Nick hoped the building would hold together for a few more days, in view of the fact that collapses were common. A maid greeted Nick and Abbi at the door; she showed them into a large, airy living room. The businessman sat propped up on a chaise lounge, his back to the open door of the terrace. A breeze gently whiffed the gauzy neutral toned curtains. The businessman's wife sat on the terrace, looking out over the city, her back to the visitors. The businessman appeared to be in his fifties. His wife was much, much younger. The maid poured tea for everyone, serving the wife on the terrace. The businessman drooled tea from his mouth. "That's OK, Boss," Abbi said, patting his napkin on the businessman's chin.

Everyone chatted amiably about the universal things one speaks of when visiting the sick. Finally, Abbi brought up the topic of the plane, the Otter. The businessman was grateful for the company and the diversion of not dwelling on his condition. He told Abbi that any friend of his was also his friend. If Abbi thought it a good idea, then let Nick use the plane. Nick sat pinching the inside of his palm. He could not believe his good fortune. "Boss, don't worry yourself about anything. If I call and you are sleeping, I will give all the details to your wife." The businessman had already nodded off to sleep. They got up to leave. The wife came into the room, wearing a beautiful silk sari and still wearing her sunglasses. She was stunning. "Thank you for coming. Please stay in touch," she said gratefully.

Nick looked at Abbi as they rode down in the elevator together and said, "The wife is a very beautiful girl, but come on, how old do you think she is?"

"I stay out of it. He's my boss and he pays well. I just enjoy the landscape," he replied.

Chapter 16

The bars at the bottom of the cage dug into her ribs as she lay on her side, exhausted. She had just given birth. She was drenched in sweat and her mouth was dry. Her body ached. The baby struggled as it searched for her breasts. The mother tried to turn in her cage. It was not sufficiently high for her to sit upright, barely long enough for her to stretch her arms and legs. The cage was so confining that she could not tell if her offspring was a male or female. To the woman's vague recollection this was the tenth child that she had borne.

Across the shed, in exactly the same crates, the female pigs groaned and nuzzled their babies; many times these mothers crushed their offspring while trying to turn over. They had no room to move. The older pigs and the three-year-old children were kept in pens together. Some of the youngsters were kept almost as pets for the workers. They kept the cutest, most precocious boys and girls that they fancied. The pigs, having the intelligence of three-year-old human children, got on well with the toddlers. The children enjoyed their time and life with the pigs, since they knew no other existence.

The women kept on these farms were bred, gave birth, milked, and immediately rebred. The off- spring of these women, were at first thought of by their captors as unwanted, but necessary by-products. Previously, the male babies, having no use financially to the farm, were immediately disposed of. They were thrown into a dumpster, and held there until they were ground up and added to meal for the livestock. Some of the ground meat was fed to the caged women and girls. With recent political, social and religious upheavals in the world, these children were now becoming valuable items of trade. Groups could purchase their future soldiers and followers; buy them at whatever age they wished and raise them with their desired beliefs and for their distinct purpose.

After the girls and women gave birth, they were immediately rebred or rather impregnated by their keepers using a "rape rack". Only a female mammal, who gives birth and is nursing will produce milk.

When the women were too old to reproduce, like the animals, they too were slaughtered. They were part of an interspecies factory farm. The women were delicacies that were highly prized on a black market that was insanely profitable. In some cultures eating the flesh of women was more erotic than having sex with them. The appetite for exotic milk and meats was growing. What was it that made drinking the milk and eating the flesh of a sentient creature so enticing?

The factory farm spread out in the valley. It was immense. The farm sat in a bowl of land, with mountains around the rim. The valley used to be very green with lush pastures and fields. Now massive shed-like structures housed thousands of animals, nonhumans and humans alike, perhaps hundreds of thousands. Feedlot pens covered the rest of the area. This was factory farming at its highest level and absolute worst. Sentient beings were everywhere. They were living and breathing one minute and a short walk later they were dead. Here they were bred, born, raised, lived, if you could call their existence living, then slaughtered, all at the same facility, at the hands of highly efficient killers, bringing to mind the actions of Rudolf Hess and Joseph Mengele. Their life in the cages was that of solitary confinement within view of others in solitary. The frustration and despair was palpable. The women and the animals in the crates shared the same thought, "Will we always be alone? Is there anyone out there to help us?"

Chapter 17

The herdsman moved his herd slowly down the mountain path. He needed warmer weather for them. The mothers with babies did not do well in the chilly early spring nights at the higher altitudes.

His was a small milking herd. There were a number of individual herdsmen who liked having their own private herd. He liked being close to his. The herdsman felt that if he raised them, nurtured them and finally slaughtered them himself, it was more humane. In the end he would look into their trusting eyes and slit their throats, their eyes turning to disbelief and then horror at being betrayed by their trusted guardian. Death quickly followed. The herdsman felt it was better that they know their slaughterer. He felt it comforting and humane.

The herdsman had purchased The Girl at auction. Many times, when the supply of women was more than the factory farm could accommodate at the moment the excess girls and women were put on the auction block. That is how The Girl found herself in this small herd of women. The herdsman was kind to all of them. They all had food, water and shelter.

He immediately took a liking to The Girl. He showered her with attention. He stroked her, petted her and spoke to her with kindness. She thought he spoke a dialect of Hindustani, but it was a dialect that she neither recognized nor spoke. With 143 dialects in India, many times the only communal language is English. She thought surely he would speak to her in a language she would understand, but it never happened.

He never really spoke to her to communicate. He just told her in an unintelligible monologue that she was a good girl, so beautiful and that he loved her so much. It dawned on her that he could not *talk to* her. He *spoke at* her. It was as if there was a species gap between the herdsmen and The Girl. He kept her tethered by a chain around her neck, set into the ground with an iron spike. It was taken out of the ground only when they moved from place to place.

He clothed the women and kept them warm and blanketed. He milked them twice a day, leaving the milk at the pre-arranged collection points. They were constantly with child. As "yearlings" he moved the babies on. Most went back to the factory farm to be disposed of at will. With The Girl's offspring, however, he could not bring himself to kill them or be passed on for someone else to kill. All her babies had beautiful eyes, some blue, some blue and brown. Over the years, he left her children in baskets at various missions presided over by Catholic nuns.

As the years passed and when the time finally came, he could not bear to kill The Girl himself. The Girl was sweet and kind to her babies. He was fascinated that she had one blue eye and one brown. She had been with him for many years. She had always been a good milk producer and easy to keep. But now she was older, a little harder to get pregnant, and not producing as much milk. He knew it was time. But he dreaded it. His only alternative was to take her back to auction. Perhaps someone would buy her. It was his only option.

Chapter 18

Many years before, when The Girl was abducted on her way home from school, she was transported to the factory farm via the infamous pig truck. There were other girls and women with her in the truck, all with their wrists bound and duct tape over their mouths and eyes. When they emerged from the underbelly of the truck they were herded into a barn, then each shoved into a holding pen. The duct tape and wrist binding were abruptly removed. The Girl blinked and rubbed her eyes and face with her hands. The sudden removal of the duct tape had pulled out most of her eyelashes and both eyebrows. She stared in horror and disbelief at the scene around her.

There were rows of cages, stacked one upon the other; the women could only lie down in them. They were like wire coffins. Most of the women had babies sucking at their breasts. On the far side of the huge shed there were iron stanchions with dozens of women and girls tethered by their necks, on each side, waiting to be milked. The smell...the smell was overwhelming to The Girl's senses, nauseating her. The women were naked, their hair filthy and matted, their bodies crusted with feces and their inner legs damp from urine.

The dejected ones were quiet. Others who screamed, had their tongues cut out. Ones who were hostile to each other were blinded or had their lips and teeth removed. Some chewed on the bars of their cages, out of utter boredom; others chewed on their inner arms until they bled. They had no activities for their bodies or their minds, day in and year out. The boredom led to hostility and self-mutilation.

Chapter 19

Nick landed the plane effortlessly in a field of early rye grass. After many days of indecision, then decision, all agreed that it was the time to try to get into the factory farm. Everyone was now well aware of what the pig trucks were really transporting and where they went. Any more time wasted was being complicit to the crimes already taking place. Both Kendra and Bryce deplaned quickly and ran for the cover of the overgrowth at the edge of the field. They walked ahead toward the first building of the huge factory farm without speaking, their thoughts their own. To the right was an old wooden shed where a dirt road came to an end.

Suddenly, Bryce was no longer the professional journalist and friend to Kendra. He had transformed into someone she didn't even presume to know. He turned to her and fumed, the words raging up from the inferno in his gut "This is MY story now. Get yourself out of here." Kendra was flummoxed, confused and hurt. She had organized this whole effort. She planted herself in front of him, not moving, glaring into his eyes with tenacious determination. Bryce picked her up by the front of her shirt and threw her against the wall of the shed. Splinters tore into the back of her left arm and shoulder. The wind had been knocked out of her. Shock and pain swelled through her body. She didn't have the strength to fight Bryce. She felt a wave of nausea come over her and she breathed hard to suppress it.

She could hear a plane engine and suddenly she remembered the ultimatum given by Nick, the pilot, when they landed in this God forsaken place. "I'll give you one hour, then I am out of here with or without you. That is it." Kendra needed to get to the airstrip. She had no idea what was going on with Bryce, but that was one variable too many for her. She pulled herself up and after a staggered start headed toward where they had landed. She reached the clearing and saw the plane starting to taxi. Her heart pounding, she screamed and ran after the plane. She was behind it. It taxied away from her, her legs not being able to run any faster. This was a dream sequence in reality: trying and trying to run faster and faster but not being able to make her feet move any faster than in slow motion. The plane got to the end of the field, turned and came back toward her. At this point she was scared that she would be run over. She lay on the dirt ready to roll one way or the other to avoid the wheels and propeller. The plane stopped abruptly only a few meters from where Kendra lay. She heard a deep authoritative voice bellow, "Get up and get in here NOW!" The cockpit door opened as she stood up and was unceremoniously hauled into the plane. "Filly, this has the smell of a nasty place and I'm glad you decided to join my flight out," Nick yelled as he throttled the engines and lifted off, skyward bound. Kendra was soaked in nervous sweat, bruised, sore and relieved to be slumped into the co-pilot's seat.

Chapter 20

This was the auction of the females. They were put in holding pens then led out into the small pen on display. With an identification number stuck on their shoulder and their hands bound, most looked resolutely down at the ground. The young ones (non-bred maidens) were auctioned off first, next the bred and confirmed pregnant, then the older barren females. It was heart wrenching to see the older females who could hardly walk, limp into the small pen. Some still had a semblance of hope rise to the surface in the irises of their eyes. Something could be seen. Yes, something was still there, although not much. These were the ones destined for slaughter. No one was here to save them. They had out lived their usefulness. The Girl was among them. This was The Girl. The herdsman saw her. His heart ached.

Bryce saw her. His heart sank. It had to be her. He could not believe it though. How could she have lasted and survived so long? The bidding started. He could have easily saved her. He could have had the highest bid. The auctioneer called for one last bid. Bryce put his hands in his pockets. She was now gone. He left his seat and walked down the steps and around the corner to the passageway leading to the holding pens. Some females were whimpering.

The worker rested the bolt gun for a moment on the metal rail, his arm weary from the constant use hour after hour. He would hold the gun to their heads, trying to get the shot directly into the temple. It was stressful and emotionally distressing to some of the workers. Others had become numb to the routine killings. The Girl moved hesitantly forward. The slaughterhouse worker raised the bolt gun, steadying his right arm with his left hand. There was a sudden sound of a latch unlocking. The metal panel directly in front of The Girl swung to block her path forward, shunting her away from the worker with the bolt gun. Moments later the thud from the bolt gun could be heard tearing into another woman's temple.

The Girl was hoisted upward and a burlap sack wrapped over and around her, covering her almost completely except for her legs. She was then tossed over the shoulders of her savior. Jerome was the least likely person for the task at hand, but he was the best visually suited, with a beard, hair in a turban and deeply bronzed skin. When later asked how he could get to her, he replied, "The workers were distributing feed. I distributed that special feed that humans crave. I threw money around, distributed it EVERYWHERE. That is all that was necessary. Nothing else mattered. I could have whatever I wanted."

His shoulders punching into her stomach with each stride, as he carried her away, The Girl wiggled and squirmed. She was trying to get him to stop. "Get my friend, too." This was all he needed, he thought, but how could he refuse. Jerome unlatched the cage The Girl was pointing to and hurriedly pulled the other female out. He now had two women slung over his shoulders. The smell of their bodies was revolting.

Jerome had spread enough money around on his way into the factory farm that he had no trouble with his exit. Martine and Greta were waiting at the edge of the woods with the horses and, of course, the dogs. The girls were unceremoniously slung into a saddle and they all quickly trotted into the bush. The forest closed behind them.

This was Plan B in action. The idea was to have another escape route. The plane had been Plan A and that had quickly deteriorated to Plan B, which was escape by horseback. Martine, Greta and Jerome had come across the mountain on horseback with the dogs a day earlier. Martine's experience in the Trans-Mongolian Horse Race made crossing the mountain at a snail's pace a cinch for her. Greta also was a rider, who frequently hacked out with her dogs at home. However, to Jerome this was a new and not so thrilling undertaking. Everyone knew full well that if it weren't for his and Kendra's long and enduring friendship, Jerome's butt would not be in a saddle or even on a horse. Each also traveled with photocopies of their passports and cash (both rupees and US dollars) in a waterproof plastic bag duct taped to their torsos.

The return trail across the mountain narrowed and twisted around a huge rock. Suddenly a rogue band of young men stepped from behind the rock, effectively blocking the trail for the horses and riders. Everyone on horseback held their collective breaths. This was one of the roving bands of unemployed, uneducated men and boys they had all heard of, the ones who sexually assault women and girls at random. The victims were simply in the wrong place at the wrong time. The attackers had no real ax to grind with women; they were lashing out at their own disappointing lots in life.

Jerome was about to die from sheer terror. Luckily the boys were not armed. They smirked and laughed as they approached the women on horseback. There were five assailants. There were three dogs, who sensed the tension and stood transfixed upon the attackers. They were just waiting for the command from Greta. She gave it. Each dog leapt upon the closest boy, forcing him to the ground. There was growling, screaming and biting. Three boys were now tangled with the dogs. The other two, seeing that the odds were against them, ran as fast as they could back down the trail. They put as much distance as they could between themselves and the dogs.

Greta yelled at Martine and Jerome to get out of there with the girls. She waited until they were out of sight, and then called the dogs off. Each boy was a whimpering, bloody mess. This was a reversal of misfortune for them. The women they encountered were usually the ones left in this condition. Greta cantered off in the direction Martine and Jerome had taken, the dogs following closely behind her. Within minutes she caught up with them. They all moved on quickly without a word.

To everyone's relief, from that point on, the ride over the mountain was uneventful. When they reached an open field, they searched for the next segment of the escape route and hoped that their support people were where they were supposed to be. Kendra had orchestrated the rescue. Without technology and a lot of luck, they would have been lost.

Two riders in polo gear on polo ponies approached. A stake truck with high sides followed closely behind. The horses that Greta, Martine, Jerome and the girls had been riding were collected by the polo players and ponied off next to their horses. The dogs, Jerome, Greta, Martine, The Girl and her friend piled quickly into the old stake truck and pulled burlap sacks over themselves. They coughed and sneezed and their eyes watered because of the dust in the burlap. The ponies went in the direction of a tea plantation and the truck headed straight for an abandoned airstrip.

Nick, piloting the Otter, was anticipating the arrival of the precious cargo. He circled the plane, tipped its wings to signal he had spotted them below, and landed. The Girl and her friend were hurriedly bundled onto the plane and strapped into their seats. Once everyone else and the dogs were on board, Oscar hurriedly slammed the airplane door shut. Nick increased the throttle and taxied down the potholed, bumpy and overgrown abandoned runway. The passengers were bounced around, but grateful to be onboard. The plane was quickly airborne. Nick would fly them south to Mumbai, leave Greta and the dogs, then fly overnight to Perth.

It had been collectively decided that Martine, Veronica and Jerome would accompany The Girl to Perth to re-unite with her mother Celia. Greta would take the dogs back to the States with her. They had been too loyal and smart to abandon to an unknown future, an alternative she could never even consider.

Veronica was the logistics person. As soon as everyone had left for the factory farm, she went to Mumbai. She carried the travel credentials for all, including the dogs, plus the dog crates, all empty, except of course, for the one full of the Pannini Puppies and their mother. She also took clean clothes and perfume for everyone. She was to simply wait at the airport in Mumbai until she got the call that they had arrived there safely.

Chapter 21

Kendra went back to the apartment. She felt terribly alone, no friends, no dogs, absolutely no one. The apartment was hollow and empty without the chaos of the puppies. They had gone with Veronica just before the factory farm raid. They would travel to the States with the other dogs, traveling as cargo accompanying racehorses flying out of Mumbai. Greta felt the puppies were old enough to withstand the trip, and they would live with her when she reached home.

Kendra couldn't relax, but she knew she needed to soak her back and shoulder in Epsom salts so that the splinters wouldn't fester and become infected. She was applying hot compresses to herself when her cell phone rang. It was Greta.

She effusively gave Kendra the good news that all were safe and well. Everyone had come out alive and unharmed. Greta and the dogs were at the Mumbai Airport Cargo Terminal, where she was organizing their transport. Nick had found her room on a flight with horses bound first for Hong Kong, the home of the Hong Kong Jockey Club, then on to Los Angeles. Nick had originally promised her he would fly directly back from Perth to help her with the dogs. She was taken aback by his generous offer and rather fancied his assistance and attention. However, he now thought it best they all leave India as soon as they possibly could, to avoid any possible retribution from anyone connected with the factory farm.

Veronica, Martine, The Girl and her friend would be landing in Perth at dawn. Greta asked if Kendra felt comfortable and safe by herself in Delhi with no one else around, especially without the dogs. Kendra assured her that she was fine and would be leaving tomorrow morning and not to worry. Greta urged her to leave the apartment and go back to the Imperial Hotel where they had special accommodations for women traveling alone. By the time they got off the phone, Kendra was convinced that Greta was probably right. Being physically and mentally exhausted would make her prone to poor decisions and even weaker judgment, making her more vulnerable and perhaps putting her in the wrong place at the wrong time.

She packed up the last of her things, looking around the apartment for anything that she or the others had missed. The place was a bit of a mess, but this was no time to worry about getting the deposit back. She had called a taxi which was waiting at the curb as she exited the apartment. A short ride later her taxi drew up in front of the hotel. While paying the driver and collecting her bags, out of the corner of her eye, a man caught her attention. He was just disappearing into a cab. Something was familiar about him, she thought. She dismissed it and continued into the hotel.

Kendra went up to her room. She had phone calls to make and numerous loose ends to tie up. Veronica's friend at the French Embassy had to be contacted to help expedite all of them getting through airport security and immigration, since none of them looked like their passport photographs. Luckily now there were iris scans and fingerprints.

She exhaled audibly and said aloud to herself, "It is finally over. We did what we set out to do!"

But, who was that in the taxi? Even more concerning was why was it gnawing at her. She got back to the matters at hand. "Just focus," she told herself. She then picked up the phone and ordered room service. She did not feel like being fawned over by overly accommodating waiters. She just wanted to have dinner, some wine and get on with things. She knew she had to contact Bryce, a task she was dreading. Kendra now knew she was beyond tired when she found her decision-making abilities at odds with each other as to whether to take a bath first or order dinner. She shook her head in utter amazement. Choices. For hundreds of women and girls at the factory farm there isn't even such a thing as a choice. She felt good about what they had all accomplished.

Kendra knew she had to eventually speak to Bryce, but she wanted to speak to Valdez first. She needed an infusion of positive energy. He picked up on the fourth ring.

"Are you OK? The human factory farm story is on the news all over the world, on every channel, network and website," he burst out breathlessly upon answering the phone.

"I'm fine. Really, I'm fine. Very lucky," Kendra replied.

"Your name isn't mentioned anywhere, though. Unless I missed it."

"No, you didn't miss anything, there is no mention of anyone except Bryce. Maybe in the long run it is best. We were actually all very lucky for everyone to get out in one piece, unharmed and alive. I had no idea what I was getting everyone into. What a nightmare."

"You probably are a bit in shock and a little traumatized," he added. "I am really all right compared to what those women and girls were going through."

"I'll be in London for a conference in two weeks. Have lunch with me," Valdez said. The mere thought of getting herself ready and anywhere in time for lunch was too much for her, too exhausting. "No, not lunch, I can only do dinner. It is a long story. And I will tell you the real story, NOT the one the media is carrying."

"Tell me, what can I bring you when I come to see you? What do you want or need?" he asked.

Kendra replied, "I don't really need anything, I can't think of anything at the moment. I am OK. I'm fine...but, I'm just thinking...on second thought. Besides getting out of here as quickly as possible the only thing in the world I need is a cat back at my cottage. That is it...I need a cat. Can you help me find a ginger cat?"

Chapter 22

Later in the evening, Kendra put a call through to Bryce. He answered. There was the sound of music in the background and ice cubes being added to a glass. "Sorry, I seem to be interrupting a party," she said unapologetically.

"Oh, heavens no, we were just wrapping things up over here, and off to bed early to catch a flight home tomorrow."

"Yes, I'm out of here tomorrow, too," said Kendra. She realized they would be on the same plane to London. "We can talk tomorrow then," he said and abruptly hung up.

"Oh God, help me. Give me patience," Kendra said to herself. She hated having to look forward to having any contact with Bryce.

The gnawing sensation that she had when she exited the taxi returned to her. What was going on? She picked up her cell phone and tapped in Jerome's number. He eventually answered.

"Hola," answered Jerome in a rather sing song happy voice.

"Where the hell are you?" demanded Kendra.

"Listen, you know I love you, but, I took matters into my own hands for a change, and changed my plans. Well, our plans. I realized the girls and Nick could handle everything between here and Perth, so I decided to come back to Delhi."

"I'm listening."

"I had to stay. He wanted me to stay. I wanted to stay with him. He is the most compelling, attractive, intelligent, sexiest, person I have ever met."

"And would this idol have a name?"

"Bryce."

Chapter 23

Fifteen years ago Bryce had put up a good facade and looked for his daughter when she disappeared, and he had found her. But, rescue her he didn't. Whether it was his daughter, or an animal to be slaughtered, his non-concern was the same. It was his lack of caring and insensitivity that was reprehensible. He was long past the point of having any sympathy about anyone except himself. He was not sure when he had become so callous. He felt sorry for himself. He had lived in denial and felt his wife had taken him for granted for years and he was played for the fool. He always found a reason and someone else to blame for any and all of his shortcomings. Then again, perhaps the fault lay in being in such close and constant proximity to the squalor, the corruption, and the brutality toward women, animals, and other defenseless beings. Perhaps that had numbed him. Nothing meant anything to him except the money that was offered to him to keep his mouth closed about the existence of the human factory farms and to leave India. He gladly took it. The money was deposited quarterly for him in an account on the Isle of Man. Bryce grew to enjoy taking long weekends there to collect his blood money.

After the raid orchestrated by Kendra on the factory farm, Bryce went back to his opulent room in the Imperial Hotel to write an exposé on the inhumanity of human factory farms. If he did not do it immediately, Kendra would. Even if he could not bring himself to save his own daughter he felt he owed it to himself to write about her and the hundreds, if not thousands of other young women who had had their lives stripped from them. This was a great story and it had to be told. He wished however, that this news did not have to come from him, but he refused to let Kendra have the story.

When the inhumane treatment of these women stopped, he knew his money would stop. Someone had to stand up for them; he just wished that he was not the one to have to do it. He could say all the right things, even if he was not saying them for the right reasons. He knew this was the best story of his life. This was THE EXCLUSIVE story of all time. Bryce filed the story under his by-line, taking full credit and responsibility for everything, as if no one else had been involved. He shared nothing. The only reason Bryce was even acknowledging the existence of the human factory farms was because he had been unable to lead Kendra off track or deter her from the investigation. He had offered to help Kendra solely to cover any involvement on his part. He had hoped he could steer her to the Cages of Bombay. However, that had not happened. He had to manipulate this situation to his benefit. If he did not write this story, she would. He had to beat her to it. IT WAS HIS, ALL HIS! The freedom for the girls was simply a fortuitous by-product of the news articles shedding light on the horror that lurked inside the factory farms.

Chapter 24

Abbi, the company pilot, made all the arrangements for Nick to take the plane. He had made numerous trips to the apartment dealing almost exclusively with the businessman's wife. Nick had put off taking the plane until Kendra's rescue mission was in place. He spent less time at the airport, saying they were wrapping up their visits with friends. They purchased some diving gear just for effect and stored it in the plane.

The Otter was old, but in good condition and its engines purred like kittens. Nick felt like he was in love. It would take a while to hopscotch their way across the eastern Indian Ocean since they would have to make fuel stops. He had laid out a route that was the most direct, but accessible to fuel. He thought it should take them about 15 hours, barring any delays or incidents. He refused to use the word accident. He outfitted the plane with everything he could think of that they might require. He secured life preservers and a life raft, shark repellent, sunscreen and blankets.

"Ladies, this is your captain speaking, welcome aboard. This will be a more or less nonstop flight to Perth, Australia. If your destination is other than Perth, please come forward and deplane now." He couldn't resist that statement. "The flight should take 15 hours. There seems to be a bit of heavy weather coming in from the east off the South China Sea; it may produce some chop, but I'll get us above it as quickly as possible. I hope to have you in Perth by lunchtime tomorrow. I wish I had a stew on board for you, but I don't, so you will have to be happy with the baskets of sandwiches and thermoses just behind the fore bulkhead. Please use the lavatory for your class of travel only...sorry, again couldn't help myself. Ok ladies, fasten your seat belts and let's get this party going!" Everyone needed and appreciated a little jocularity after what they had just been through.

Veronica and Martine tucked the girls into their sleeping bags and fastened their seat belts around them. The women investigated the food baskets and decided on just black tea for the moment. They settled back in their seats and listened to the roar of the engines. Soon everyone in the cabin was asleep.

The Girl and her friend were comfortable; they awoke a few times during the flight, mostly during the landings and take-offs for refueling, and then snuggled down again with blankets over their heads. Nick had been most considerate and thoughtful in outfitting the plane with warm blankets, pillows, sleeping bags and food for the trip from Mumbai.

Martine awoke in the middle of the night, quietly contemplating and gazing out the window at nothing. She was thinking about what had just transpired in the last day, about the girls they had with them and the girls and women at the factory farm. There was some turbulence. Once calm had resumed, Martine unbuckled her seatbelt and got up to use the lavatory. She pulled on the door, but it would not open. She tried the handle again. She went forward to get Oscar's assistance. "Just turn it," he said.

"I've tried. I think it's locked," said Martine.

"It can't be."

"Well it is," she sighed.

Oscar went aft to try his hand at the lock. "That's odd, the handle doesn't move at all," said Oscar. "Let me get a screw driver."

Using the screwdriver, Oscar removed the lavatory door handle and pulled the door open.

"Holy crap!" he exclaimed.

"Nick, you've got to come here, quick," he continued.

Nick put the plane on autopilot and went aft. He could not believe what he saw in the lavatory. There stood the businessman's wife.

He brought her forward into the cockpit and put her in the co-pilot's seat. Over the next hours she told her story. She kept begging Nick not to take her back to Delhi. That indeed was the last thing on his mind. She explained that she had been a virtual sex slave to the businessman; he passed her off as his wife. Missionary nuns in the countryside had raised her and she had no idea who her parents were or what had happened to them. One day about a year ago, while shopping at a local market fair, she was abducted and delivered to the apartment of the businessman. She thought she was about fourteen years old at the time.

Dawn was starting to peep over the eastern horizon. Sunlight entered the cockpit. Nick reached over and removed the sunglasses of the businessman's wife, revealing one blue eye and one brown.

The landing in Perth was smooth and uneventful. Martine and Veronica leaned over to rouse the girls. Martine gently pulled the covers back on each sleeping bag, expecting to expose sleepy heads. The Girl's friend blinked and squinted at the bright sunshine streaming into the cabin through the small windows. She turned to look at The Girl. Her sleeping bag was empty. The Girl was not there. Martine and Veronica stared at each other in disbelief and abject horror. Nick came back into the cabin. He too stared in disbelief at the empty seat.

"Where is she?"

"Where did she go?"

"How did she leave?"

"When did she leave?"

"We never opened the cabin door when we were refueling."

"Who could have taken her?"

"It is as if she never existed!"

"Gone without a trace."

"What do we tell Celia?"

"The truth."

"Kendra is the one I don't want to face," sighed Nick.

Celia was waiting for the plane at the private aviation terminal as planned. Veronica realized she had to be the grownup, face Celia and simply tell her what had transpired; not that she actually knew what had happened. Celia listened to the saga, the turn of events, the escape, and the plane ride and finally the disappearance of her daughter. Celia's response was to the point, however unexpected.

"Perhaps now, we can all be free."

At the top of the gangway, the businessman's "wife" slowly emerged from the darkness of the airplane. Celia at first looked confused, slowly processing what was taking place. Then she began to cry tears of joy.

Chapter 25

Bryce and Kendra sat opposite each other in the airport lounge, each drinking a gin and tonic. "This is the only way to beat this heat," he said. " I think the Brits invented the drink just for here. Think they used straight quinine water early on. Perhaps a possible cure for Malaria."

Ignoring his comment Kendra looked him straight in the eye, saying, "You knew exactly where she was all along, didn't you? How could you have been such a heartless bastard? To your own daughter no less."

"First of all, The Girl is not my daughter; I never had a daughter, you must realize that. And for that matter, neither did Celia. She has been in denial for years that she had a miscarriage. I have no idea who the father was. This imaginary daughter of hers took on a life of her own; she even imagined that she was kidnapped. This is the perfect example of the manifestation of self-denial. But, when did you realize I knew about the factory farm?" he replied.

"When you repeatedly tried to steer our search down to the Cages in Bombay, when we were witnessing the trafficking going north. Then it became quite obvious when you slammed me against the wall of that shed at the factory farm. That went through me loud and clear."

"I'm sorry about that," he said, never looking her in the eye.

"Years ago Celia was distraught and her denial took on a materiality in her mind. She put up such a fuss that to placate her I said I would look for The Girl. Besides I thought there might be a story in it. Then I happened, by chance, upon the factory farm. The owners of the factory farm and I came to an agreement. It was less messy than their killing me. Let me say, they made me an offer I couldn't refuse. All I had to do was go away and say nothing to anyone. I acquiesced, and quite frankly the amount of money they offered was unbelievable, insanely unbelievable. I could not refuse it. I felt I owed it to myself. It changed my life. I could have anything I wanted, anytime I wanted it. And now, with this story, I will have everything I've dreamed of professionally. The whole exposé, you've seen it on the news, you saw how the story was received; people can't get enough of it. This could lead to a Pulitzer. Just imagine it. I bet movie offers will follow," he bragged.

"And you think the owners of the human factory farm will let you just walk all over them?" Kendra asked.

"Well, I'm doing it, aren't I? Do you see anyone stopping me? The money I will make from the story and perhaps the movie is worth every bit of the risk," he replied.

He sickened Kendra. Boarding was called. She got up and headed to the departure gate. She kept telling herself Bryce was a non-entity, an ignorant, self-absorbed, selfish moron who did not amount to anything in the scheme of the Universe. All that mattered was that The Girl had been found and freed from that human factory farm. In fact all the women, girls and children had been rescued. It was over. Bryce's news story burst the whole human factory farming business wide open. It was over, for now, until the next greed-ridden scheme against women arose. You cannot change a culture overnight, not even in a decade, hopefully in a century a nano-percentage of change would be evident.

Kendra slumped in her seat; her head pressed on the hard border of the airplane's window, staring out at endless nothing. She felt so despondent. Her thoughts kept going back to William Hogarth's prints, *The Four Stages of Cruelty*. The mentality toward women and the factory farm was the coming to life of these centuries old lithographs. The heinous acts by the men running the factory farm were far more unsettling to her than she could ever imagine. She wondered if the girls and women who survived might ever become whole again.

The fact that they could have located these girls was a sheer miracle. They had incredible luck and tenacity on their side. Each had ideas as to who the businessman's wife was. Celia now had flat mates, The Girl's friend, and the businessman's wife, who actually came with a dowry. The Otter was easily worth

$300,000.00 US dollars when sold. The Australian Immigrations and Customs people would have their hands full and be busy for quite awhile.

Chapter 26

Kendra walked up to the luggage carousel at Heathrow Airport. Bryce and Jerome had deplaned ahead of her, since they had flown first class and she coach. They got to the carousel a minute or so before and walked around to where the bags were entering. She heard a strange thud, like a muffled shot, and then saw Bryce crumple to the floor of the baggage area. Jerome took a few seconds to process what was happening. He saw blood oozing from Bryce's chest. He was horrified. Kendra and Jerome's eyes met. She mouthed to him, "L-E-T'S G-O…!!"

She caught sight of her bag out of the corner of her eye, took hold of it, immediately turned on her heal and proceeded through Customs, under the green light labeled "Nothing to Declare."

About the Author

<u>Judith Mazzucco</u>

Judith, an interdisciplinary artist, works in mixed media, film, photography and words. Her praxis investigates interspecies relationships and the marginalizing effect of domestication on animals and the consequential effect upon creativity. An art educator, Monmouth University alumna, she received her M.F.A. in New Media, Transart Institute, Danube University, Austria. Judith exhibits her visual processes nationally and internationally. She can be found most frequently with her collaborators of various species, in her studio, the aisle of the barn, on her farm in New Jersey.

www.judymazzucco.com

Cover design: Judith Mazzucco   *Author's photo: Pablo Maitia*

Made in the USA
Columbia, SC
06 December 2022

72374032R00037